"You!" Elinore pointed her blade at Malcolm.

"Help me with his armor, since you are the only man without work to do."

"You despise my idleness?" He chuckled, deep and as intriguing as midnight.

"That and more. Now quickly. I must see the wound. Use my blade." She jabbed the knife toward him, hilt first.

His big, blunt-shaped fingers curled over the steel weapon, engulfing it. The thick blade appeared like a toy against his size and dark, lethal power. She read the cynical darkness in his eyes, hated the strength in his rock-hewn body. The latent power to kill rested in the thickness of his arms and shoulders, chest and thighs.

Malcolm both took her breath away and made her blood run cold. He was a beautiful masculine form. He was a destroyer of life. The irony beat at her.

Truly this was the epitome of man…!

Dear Reader,

The perfect complement to a hot summer day is a cool drink, some time off your feet and a good romance novel. And we have four terrific stories this month for you to choose from!

Jillian Hart made her writing debut in our 1998 March Madness Promotion with her outstanding Western, *Last Chance Bride*. The same emotional and gently passionate style she's developed in her Westerns is ever present in *Malcolm's Honor,* Jillian's first medieval romance. Set in England, it's the story of Malcolm the Fierce, a loyal knight who captures a noblewoman suspected of treason. When Malcolm brings her to the king, the king awards Malcolm with the woman's land…*then* forces him to marry her! Malcolm soon finds himself falling in love with his beautiful wife, but is still unsure he can trust her.…

In *Lady of Lyonsbridge* by Ana Seymour, another wonderful Medieval, an heiress falls in love with a knight who comes to her estate on his way to pay a kidnapped king's ransom. Judith Stacy returns with a darling new Western, *The Blushing Bride,* about a young lady who travels to a male-dominated logging camp to play matchmaker for a bevy of potential brides—only to find herself unexpectedly drawn to a certain mountain man of her own!

Rounding out the month is *Jake's Angel* by newcomer Nicole Foster. In this book, an embittered—and wounded— Texas Ranger on the trail of a notorious outlaw winds up in a small New Mexican town and is healed, emotionally and physically, by a beautiful widow.

Enjoy! And come back again next month for four more choices of the best in historical romance.

Sincerely,

Tracy Farrell
Senior Editor

JILLIAN HART

MALCOLM'S HONOR

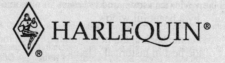

HARLEQUIN®

TORONTO • NEW YORK • LONDON
AMSTERDAM • PARIS • SYDNEY • HAMBURG
STOCKHOLM • ATHENS • TOKYO • MILAN • MADRID
PRAGUE • WARSAW • BUDAPEST • AUCKLAND

ISBN 0-373-29119-1

MALCOLM'S HONOR

This edition published by arrangement with Harlequin Books S.A.

® and TM are trademarks of the publisher. Trademarks indicated with
® are registered in the United States Patent and Trademark Office, the
Canadian Trade Marks Office and in other countries.

Visit us at www.eHarlequin.com

Printed in U.S.A.

Available from Harlequin Historicals and
JILLIAN HART

Last Chance Bride #404
Cooper's Wife #485
Malcolm's Honor #519

Please address questions and book requests to:
Harlequin Reader Service
U.S.: 3010 Walden Ave., P.O. Box 1325, Buffalo, NY 14269
Canadian: P.O. Box 609, Fort Erie, Ont. L2A 5X3

Chapter One

On the road to Dover, 1280

"By the rood, we have company."

Lady Elinore of Evenbough turned at the sound of her protector's voice. The tall knight, harsh as the night was long, did not seem alarmed at the cluster of men drawing closer along the forest road, only amused.

"'Tis thieves. Look how slow they ride," her father said with a laugh. "Luck is with us. We have been journeying for a good part of a sennight and still no sign of Edward's knights."

"Do not speak of luck, my lord." The knight took hold of his sword. "Nor believe the king will forget your transgressions."

"Yours, as well."

Elin considered her father's words. He had told her little the night he'd interrupted her dreams, rousing her with only a shake of her shoulder and a stern order to dress to ride. Was the castle under attack? Mayhap an illness? Her questions had gone unanswered. She had packed a sack of clothing and two small crocks of herbs, and joined her father in the bailey.

There had been only a handful fleeing that night, if indeed they were fleeing. Three of Father's most trusted knights, and her elderly chaperon, Alma, who had cared for Elin since birth. Father had bidden them to remain silent as he'd led the way down the shadowed road. It had been thus for four nights, traveling beneath the cloak of a new moon, keeping out of the sight of travelers brave enough to risk the dangerous roads after midnight.

Now it seemed their luck had turned. Elin bit back questions she dared not ask her father, a harsh and severe man—questions about why one loyal and close to the king would need to hide in the darkness.

"Thieves can be easily dealt with," Alma whispered in her ear. "But methinks those are knights. Look how black they are, for there is no moon to gleam off their mail. Were they thieves, they would wear even a small amount of colored cloth."

"Quiet, old woman," her father's knight ordered.

Had they not been in such danger, Elin would have spoken. No matter his worth as a warrior, Brock could improve his manners, especially toward the elderly.

"By the blood, they are knights." Father's voice resonated with a hollow sound—fear, mayhap. Or something worse.

"Many knights," Alma whispered again.

Elin's grip tightened on the reins. Without doubt, there would be a battle and much danger. She had learned long ago to think of her own safety, for her father had little concern for her or Alma's welfare. In truth, why he'd brought her with him remained a mystery. Since her brother's death in the Crusades while fighting at Edward's side, the mere sight of Elin angered her sire.

"Come." She spoke low and touched Alma's cloak. "We must hide."

A battle was no place for unarmed women. Had Father allowed her, she would not hesitate to carry a sword for protection. Her hand crept to the knife she kept at her girdle. She was not helpless. And any man foolish enough to believe so would discover how fine a warrior she could be.

"Dismount," Elin instructed when the forest proved too dense for the great horses. It mattered little if they were on foot. She had all she needed—a weapon in hand and the cloak of darkness. "Father will chase off those arrogant knights. Look how they challenge him."

"Do not be so certain," Alma warned. "See that big knight, the one atop the black stallion? He is Malcolm le Farouche. Malcolm the Fierce."

"The king's protector? You must be mistaken, Alma. What could Father have done to bring the king's men after him?"

"Treason."

"Nay, it cannot be. Father is loyal to the king."

"Your father is loyal to gold coin."

Elin could not argue that truth. She had long witnessed that flaw in her father's character. His love of money had nearly been the ruin of the barony. His conscience did not so much as twinge at the thought of others going hungry in order to feed his greed. But treason?

"Put down your sword, Baron Philip of Evenbough, by command of the king," the black knight ordered.

"I trust you not, Farouche. You have long been known for your dubious misdeeds." Father's sword slid from its scabbard, a sound of metal upon leather in the still night. "I command *you,* le Farouche, to put down your arms and let us go as peaceable men."

"Since when are a murderer's deeds peaceable?"

Elin could see the knight's great gleaming darkness as, clothed in shadows, he lifted his sword. Malcolm the

Fierce. His voice came as sharp as his sword, hard as his name. She could see broad shoulders, wider than she'd noticed on any man, and the power of his arm. Painted in shades of night, he led the charge.

"No!" She could not hold back the cry that tore from her throat. Her hiding place revealed, she slapped her hand to her mouth. But she remained unnoticed as the clash of sword upon sword and the blood cry of battling men filled the forest. She could smell the sweat of horses, the fresh musk of upturned earth beneath their hooves and the sharp scent of blood.

"Down, girl." Alma's hand curled in the fabric of her sleeve. Not until that moment was Elin aware she'd risen to her feet.

She knelt back in the shadows, her fingers growing clammy around the hilt of her dagger. Violence frightened her, but something terrified her even more.

It came as a whisper in her mind, a shimmer of foreboding as intangible as the night. Her father would lose this battle. Had King Edward's knights tracked them from Evenbough to kill or capture them? Or was Father right? Was le Farouche working against the king for his own vile agenda? Either was possible. There had been rumors, aye; there were always rumors. But as flawed as her father was, Elin found it hard to believe him capable of murder. And yet—

"We must escape whilst we can," Alma whispered, her voice raspy from age and fear. "Come. That is Brock who has fallen. There, on the ground by the lee side of that boulder. Do you see him?"

"Aye." Cold hard fear clenched Elin's belly. Brock had failed to stop the dark knight, Malcolm the Fierce.

"They may not know we are here," Elin said. "If we attempt to move, they may spot us."

"Not in the heat of battle." Alma tugged hard on Elin's cloak and, stooping so as not to disturb tree boughs, took a small step. "Those knights are no fools. They are the best in the realm, chosen by Edward himself. They will count the bodies—"

"Then count the horses, and come looking for us," Elin finished. "We have no choice. We must run. Quietly, now."

A twig snapped. The fingers gripping her cloak let go. Was she alone? The dark shadows beneath the trees made it impossible to see. "Alma?"

Cold metal touched her throat, and then a hard male hand gripped her shoulder with crushing force. Sinew and bone bruised beneath those mighty fingers, and Elin cried out. "Where is Alma? She's an old woman. If you hurt her, you devil's spawn, I shall make you pay."

Male laughter rang above the sounds of the forest. "God's teeth, a warrior woman. I truly quake in fear."

She jabbed her elbow backward and struck chain mail and immovable man. Let him jest. She had not yet begun to fight. She lifted her right hand and slashed at the hard male fist holding a knife to her throat. She hit a steel gauntlet and did no harm. "Fie!"

More laughter. "Easy, little dove. I do not hurt women."

Before Elin could stop him, he'd stripped the knife from her grip and lifted her into the air. She fell hard against the jagged surface of his mail. It bit into her flesh and she cried out again. When she kicked, trying to flee, he held her more tightly to his chest. Such a broad, unyielding chest.

"Set me down." She would not allow this man or any man to ravish her. Not without a fight. If only she had her knife. "Set me down, cowardly knave."

"As you wish."

Her feet touched ground, and she saw her father. She

twisted away from the dark knight's steely grip, running toward the old man who knelt on the bloodstained road, head bowed. "Father. You're hurt."

"Wrongly accused is more like it," he growled, anger fueling his voice.

Elin knelt beside him. "You've a cut to your head." She reached to better inspect the wound, but steel wrapped around her wrist.

The great black knight stared down at her, and they glared at one another, eye-to-eye. Even in the shadows she could measure the power of the man, the strength and cunning that all should fear.

But she would not. "Are you proud of your deeds? You've injured an old man and kidnapped an old woman. What a brave warrior."

She saw darkness in those hard eyes, a glint of warning. "Do not fool with me, maiden. I strike with the authority of the king. If you have more to say, then tell it to Edward."

"Nay, I—"

"Silence," he hissed through clenched teeth. His voice was low and dangerous.

No good would come from pushing one so fierce. But Elin was not through with him. Not by far.

"The old woman you speak of is safe with the horses." The dark knight raised his sword. "Prepare for travel. We have a long ride this night."

Elin met his gaze, already hating this man of war and violence who had used brute force to carry her from the woods and who now raised a sword against her father.

What knight was he who made the weak and the old cower before him? Well, Elin would not cower. She was not weak or frightened.

But as she allowed another knight to help her onto her

palfrey, she knew she ought to be afraid of the man of darkness, of Malcolm le Farouche.

Malcolm looked down at the baron, wounded and dishonored. Had Philip of Evenbough committed another crime, Edward may have found some way… Nay, regardless of rank, a grave punishment awaited the man. Philip would pay with his life for killing Edward's cousin.

Now, what was to become of the girl? She ought to be safe in a husband's bed, not journeying along dangerous roads with a traitor. A thorough search revealed only enough food to see the party to the coast, but no gold. Passage to Normandy had its price. Either the girl had been brought along to be sold, or Evenbough had a supply of hidden coin.

Was she innocent or criminal? Had she known of her father's actions? She was young, between fifteen and twenty summers, he wagered, and weighed little more than a child. Yet she was not helpless, as she appeared. The traitor's daughter was no peaceful dove.

"Bind him," Malcolm instructed his men, pointing his sword at the dishonored Evenbough. "We take him alive to the king, as ordered."

"And the women?"

He remembered the knife, now in his possession, and recalled how the maiden had wielded it with skill. "Bind them, but do not strike them. And take care not to tie the old one too tightly. Tell her that if she escapes, I will take her charge's life. She will believe me."

Malcolm the Fierce had killed many and often. Even now three more bodies littered the road. But none were his men, of that he made sure. He worked them hard so in battle they would not be defeated, would not lose their lives carrying out the orders of a fickle king. What was justice in a world ruled by men? They were easily led astray by gold, power and women. Malcolm sighed. He'd seen too much in the Crusades, fighting for a cause he no longer believed in. He no longer believed in any cause.

"Unhand me, you knave." The girl's voice rang with a bold fury.

"Ow," Hugh cried.

Malcolm gave more orders to his men and, certain he would be obeyed, strode to the horses, arriving in time to see the traitor's daughter land a mighty kick on the young knight's shoulder.

"Cease, maiden. Or I shall be forced to treat you in a like manner." Malcolm wrapped his hand around her slim ankle, preventing further abuse to his knight.

"You bade me not to strike her," Hugh explained as he rubbed his shoulder. "Though I am sorely tempted."

"I admire your restraint." Malcolm laughed as the female tried to kick her way free from his steely grip. "Behave, maiden, else I will let Hugh have his way with you."

"Ha! As if I would want one such as this," the knight replied. "Give me a soft woman who knows naught of fighting, but much of loving."

Malcolm bade the young knight to tend the old woman, while the girl, mounted on the gray palfrey, seethed with silent fury. Decisions must be made. The journey ahead was long and brought with it danger, even for the best knights in the realm.

"If I release hold of your foot, will you cease this unruly behavior?"

"Mayhap." Shadows shaped her face and cloaked it, too. He could not read her intent, but he heard the lie in her voice.

Ah, so she was not as skilled a criminal as her father. Perhaps she was innocent. 'Twas not his place to judge.

"Your ankle is finely shaped and delicate, but I am not fooled by your small size. Tell me, warrior maiden, do you carry another knife?"

"Nay. You took my only one."

"And there is not another hidden beneath your mantle?"

"Why do you doubt me, Sir Cowardly Knight? I speak the truth."

He caught sight of her chin, a chiseled curve of both silk and defiance.

"Then you will not protest if I search for more of your weaponry. A king's knight must take precautions."

"A king's knight should not attack innocent travelers and force them to his will. I think you are not so brave, sirrah."

"'Tis not your regard I seek," he retorted with a laugh. The maiden had the fire of a young mare, not yet tamed or ridden by man. "My loyalty is to the king. Only his opinion matters. And he wishes Evenbough and all who accompany him delivered to his court. You chose the company of a traitor. Do not blame me."

"I am no more a traitor than you. Mayhap less of one."

"Watch yourself, maiden, else I may be forced to treat you more harshly. But I am not yet cruel. Here is your choice. Either I search for the knives you keep hidden beneath your mantle, or I bind you like a prisoner."

Her mouth clamped shut. He could see the generous cut of her lips, bow shaped and tempting. 'Twould be a sad day when Malcolm le Farouche was tempted by any woman.

"I would rather be bound by chains than have a cowardly knight disrobe me."

"We agree." For even the sight of a woman's bare, silken curves could never entice more than lust from him, and even then, a fleeting lust.

He was, as they said, the fiercest of knights, void of conscience, void of passion. A man without heart or soul.

"Mount up, we ride," he commanded, and bound the woman's wrists.

Chapter Two

"Take care how you speak," Alma whispered while they rode side by side. Their horses were led by the knight called Hugh, who kept a careful eye on the position of Elin's feet. "'Twould not be good to tempt Malcolm le Farouche's anger."

"He is a villain."

"He strikes with the authority of the king. We are at his mercy. Pray do not forget that the next time you speak to him."

"*If* I speak. I want naught to do with that cowardly knave." She could see him up ahead. He was touched by stardust now that the clouds above had parted. Though he shone with silver light, he was still more shadow than substance as he led the entourage, sword raised, an image of power and might.

"See? Again you speak without thought. I bid you to cease with the insults. Call him neither coward nor knave. You have yet to see the world as I have, little one. He has done naught but bind our wrists and your feet. Look how loosely Sir Hugh tied me. 'Tis far better than abuse and rape, so mind your tongue."

Fine. But Elin's anger grew. She was no chattel to be

bound like a cow on butchering day. Or a weakling afraid
to stand up to tyranny. Look how he rode, spine straight
and those broad shoulders gleaming with dark light. Triumph and arrogant pride held him up, no doubt. No matter
the cost, she refused to be at that knave's mercy.

"Elin, what are you about?" Alma muttered, and drew
the attention of the knight called Hugh, who kept peering
with suspicious eyes over his shoulder, despite the restric-
tion of his armor.

Surely Elin's few kicks to his chest and shoulder had
done no more than bruise him. How else was she to fight
when she had no weapons—well, none she wanted to reveal?

"I am locating my dagger," she whispered when Hugh
turned forward to watch the road.

"Toward what end? Pray do not tell me you wish to
wage war against six knights with one small blade?"

"I intend to cut our bindings, silly goose." Elin shook
her head. "I shall outwit those knights. They are far too
sure of themselves."

"As are you."

Elin frowned at Alma's wry comment. Didn't she have
every right to be furious? She was trussed up like livestock.
And worse, she had deeper fears she would not confess to
Alma. Whether true or not, her father was being taken to
the king under the charge of treason. She had at first
thought such accusations unlikely, but Father's righteous
fury changed her mind. An innocent man would not spout
death threats and then offer bribes to anyone who could
free him.

Was the dark knight correct? Would she face the same
charges just by being in her father's company? But what if
le Farouche followed his own agenda in kidnapping them?

If he'd concocted the accusations against her father, what future awaited her then?

Either way, escape seemed the best course.

As if sensing her intentions, Hugh turned to study her carefully. Grateful for the shadows of a grove they rode through, Elin froze. She tried to appear innocent until he faced forward again. Then she wiggled the knife tucked against her waist so that its hilt caught against the inside of her elbow. With a little concentration, she freed the blade from the small scabbard beneath her mantle.

So far so good. Now to retrieve it. She had to appear innocent every time Hugh turned to spy on her. That damnable knight was truly annoying.

Finally the blade slid down the length of her sleeved arm and into her palm. The sharp point nicked her flesh, but she didn't even wince. Such victory! With the way that dark knight led his men, eyes straight ahead and nose to the sky, he would never know she and Alma had slipped away into the darkness.

But Hugh would notice. Something had to be done about him.

"I see what you are up to," Alma whispered, piquing Hugh's interest once more.

"Alma! Stop this! How are we to escape if you keep drawing that annoying knight's attention?"

"We ought not to escape." Alma drew herself up straight, her low voice ringing with authority. "Listen to me for once, Elinore. They will set us free. We are innocent. Edward is a fair and just king."

"I trust no man, not even the king." And not Malcolm le Farouche. "Neither should you."

"And tell me what harm can come to two women traveling these woods unarmed and unprotected? Nothing worse than what will befall us by staying beneath the fierce knight's protection.''

Elin hated it when Alma made sense. ''I will protect you.''

''You have no sword or armor, little one. You are brave, but do not consider it. I pray you, stay with me. No harm will come to us. You wait and see.''

Now what should she do? Elin waited until Hugh faced forward again before she positioned the hilt in her palm and worked the tip of the knife into the bindings.

''Surrender your weapon, maiden warrior.'' A deep voice shivered over the back of her neck, vibrating down her spine.

She jumped. The knife fell to the ground, lost forever. Le Farouche rode half a hair's width beside her. How had he gotten there? He'd been at the lead just moments ago. He made no sound as he rode alongside her. Was he part demon? How would she fight him now?

''As you can see, I have no weapon.'' She held flat both palms. ''I speak the truth.''

''Then why do you bleed as if pricked by a sharp blade?''

'''Tis from the bindings.''

''Do not mistake me for a fool.''

She lifted her chin. ''Or me, cowardly knight.''

''Hsst!'' Alma whispered, scolding her.

The dark knight's laughter boomed through the silent forest. ''I see that at least one of you females has good sense. Listen to the older one, dove. Escape would only bring peril and prove your guilt to the king.''

''I have no guilt.'' She'd had her share of misdeeds and misadventures, but not treason. ''If you believe in our innocence, then release us.''

''And risk the king's wrath? 'Tis unlikely.''

"The king need never know."

"You are not just fierce, you're clever, not a typical maiden. I like that." His great voice thundered over her, at once powerful and kind.

Kind? Now, where had that notion come from?

He leaned close and she could smell the night scent of him, mysterious, wooded, crisp like cool air. "If I see any knives, I will seize them. Do not reveal your weapons and I will allow you to keep them."

He spurred his destrier forward, leaving her behind with the shades and shadows of night.

"'Tis twice he's forgiven your transgressions, Elin. Do not tempt his anger further," Alma murmured.

Elin cursed at the loss of her knife and felt some satisfaction that she had another tucked inside her mantle. Just one weapon left.

'Twould have to be enough.

"We are being watched," Sir Giles said in a low tone so that his voice wouldn't carry.

"That has not escaped me." Malcolm did not look around. He saw no reason to alert whoever watched them that he knew of their presence. "I sense two riders keeping just to the east of us in the wood. They ride distant enough so we hear naught of their movements but close enough to strike quickly. See how my stallion senses them."

"I hear now and then the sound of hooves on dried twigs."

Malcolm pulled off his helm. Cool damp air swept across his brow. "At least two ride west of us as well. Did you hear the sound of a horse exhaling?"

"Look how your stallion swivels his ears."

"More will be waiting on the path ahead of us. Expect an ambush. Alert the men. Quietly."

"Aye. We will fare better if we are not surprised." Giles fell back to speak to each knight in turn, giving no sign of alarm.

Malcolm slid his helm down over his face. He neither loved battle like some nor hated it like others. 'Twas something he excelled at, however. His blood heated with anticipation. His grip on his sword tightened.

"What of the women?" Hugh rode up beside Malcolm for a moment. "If you count four men, surely there will be more. I cannot sit by and watch a battle. I must fight."

"We may well be outnumbered. Leave the women to their own devices. The girl is armed."

"She mayhap could level an entire army with that kick of hers."

As a knight, one who made his way by fighting and war, Malcolm admired courage and strength in all forms. Even in a girl-woman who knew not enough of the world to be afraid of it.

"Look to. Up ahead the road narrows." The perfect spot for an ambush. Malcolm studied the lay of the land. Enormous boulders blocked his view of the shadowed lane. The stillness of the forest told him his instincts where correct. Their opponents would strike from both the front and behind, an organized charge. By whom? Why?

He drew to a halt. His men, ready to fight, positioned themselves. He heard the girl, Evenbough's daughter, demand to know why they were stopping. Then why Hugh was cutting Alma's bindings. Malcolm thought to bid her to silence, but he felt it then, the expectant charge in the air right before battle, as if nature could sense the impending clash of men and muscle and sword, and the resulting injury and death.

He lifted his shield. "Who challenges us?" he bellowed into the night.

There was no answer. "You think you have surprised us? Cowards, show your ugly faces."

No movement.

Then a stallion trumpeted in the dark, and hooves drummed upon rock and earth. Figures burst out of the brush in front of them and at their flanks. Malcolm met the first man with the might of his sword. He landed a blow to the knight's shoulder and deflected a thrust with his shield.

The crisp focus found only in battle filled his head, beat in his veins. Malcolm wheeled his stallion around and charged, knocking the knight to the ground. As another attacked him, he easily landed a bloody blow.

Not even breathing hard, he drew his mount to a halt. Blood thundered in his head. Battle cries and the clash of steel surrounded him. He counted three knights on the ground. Saw Giles in trouble and rode to his aide. Together, they fought side by side. But the two knights proved difficult to defeat. Malcolm took a bruising blow to his collarbone and another to his ribs before he felled them.

"We are sorely outnumbered," he shouted as he engaged another knight. "Look to Hugh. He's injured."

"I cannot," Giles cried as more knights descended upon him.

Malcolm spun his destrier and charged deep into the fray. He took another blow, this one to his helm. Blood filled his mouth, though 'twas hardly more than a split lip. "Behind you, Hugh!" he called, lifting his sword.

Hugh turned to face his enemy, but Malcolm could not reach his friend in time. Every galloping step of his stallion seemed in slow motion. The enemy knight evaded Hugh's shield and drove his sword deep into the young man's abdomen, breaking mail and flesh. Hugh fell bonelessly to the ground.

"No!" Malcolm cried. In an instant his sword lanced the

knight's side. He knocked away the weapon, then the shield, then dragged the knight to the ground with him. He'd found the man in charge of this attack, for this was no band of robbers. He tossed the knight against the broad trunk of a tree and held his blade to his throat. "Do you yield?"

"Not without the woman."

"Are you a fool? Attacking the king's knights? Yield, I say, or I will drag you to Edward myself."

He felt his enemy tremble. No courageous knight, this; not even a fine mercenary, but one grown soft working for some lord or baron, protecting his fences and castle walls. "I yield."

"Call off your men. Now, I say!"

"Beo! Cedric! Hold!" The enemy lifted his helm.

"Tell me your name," Malcolm demanded, the edge of his sword tight beneath the leader's throat.

"I am Caradoc of Ravenwood and I claim right to the baron's daughter."

The little dove? "Is she your wife?"

"Nay, Philip had agreed on a match between us."

"Philip is bound for the king's court, as will you be."

Even in the darkness, Ravenwood paled. "My intent was to capture the woman, Elin."

"Then you know of Evenbough's flight?"

"We tracked him."

Tight with fear, that voice. Ravenwood's body felt tense. Not with the anticipated bunch of muscles ready for a fight, but with true terror. This was no warrior. This was a man without courage.

"Pray," Ravenwood begged, "do not kill me."

Malcolm's sword hovered while he decided his course. "Bid your men to lie facedown, arms spread. We will take them as prisoners."

"Why? We want only the woman. She's a maiden, an innocent."

"A woman has no innocence." Malcolm pressed the edge of his blade to Ravenwood's throat until he drew blood. "'Tis not my place to judge your intentions or the girl's. Like you, her future will be determined by the king."

"Then you are the greater fool, Malcolm the Fierce." Ravenwood's eyes glittered in the way of men who cannot win by their battle skills, but by deceit and manipulation. "I am a favored nephew of the king. He will have your head, if I do not have it first."

"You are the fool, Ravenwood. Do not threaten one who has spared your life. Else you may not have the same fate when we meet next."

"You are not a lord, sirrah, but a hired man of the king's. A barbarian sired you, and a barbarian you will always be. I know your ilk, le Farouche, and I spit on it."

"You are a brave man with words, but you mistake my sensibilities. I know I am like my father, a killer to the bone. And knowing this should frighten you." Malcolm tightened his grip on the hilt of his sword. "Do my bidding while I am still of a mind to spare your life."

"Kill me and earn the king's disfavor." Ravenwood laughed with the cocky ease of a lord's spoiled son, born to a life of uselessness.

"I do not fear the king's disfavor." Malcolm tossed the traitor to the ground, pressed a foot to the small of his back to pin him there, and eased the sharp point of his sword into the vulnerable spot between his hauberk and the back of his helm.

"Lie on the ground or your lord will be run through," he commanded the others.

The half-dozen remaining knights eased themselves to the bloodstained earth, wary and uncertain of their fate.

"Bind them. We'll have more prisoners for Edward's dungeon." Malcolm knelt with some satisfaction to tie Caradoc of Ravenwood's hands behind his back. "Pray your uncle looks upon you with favor, for being found trying to rescue a traitor is a damning act."

"I merely wanted the shrew." Caradoc's words were muffled from the dirt in his mouth. "I will have your head, le Farouche, one way or another."

"You are not warrior enough to win it in a fight." Malcolm did not value his head overmuch. "I will gag you as well. I grow tired of your threats."

Malcolm stood careful watch while Caradoc of Ravenwood and his bound men were chained to trees like dogs.

"You did not take his head," Giles observed. "You have taken far more from those who have insulted you less."

"He is a relative of the king and a powerful man."

"You are afraid?" Giles's astonished whisper carried in the still night air.

"Nay, but wary. I never turn my back on a serpent." He'd seen the contrivances of men like Caradoc and had recognized in his manner a man who took triumph in hurting others. "Is Hugh dead?"

"Mortally wounded." Giles gestured toward the road, where their men had gathered. "We lost no others."

"And the women?"

"Escaped during the fray. Shall I track them?"

"The king will be displeased if we do not." His thoughts turning to the wounded man, Malcolm raced across uneven ground toward the fallen knight. Men parted to allow room at Hugh's side. Silence and sorrow scented the air.

Grief tore at Malcolm's heart as he knelt, knowing he was helpless to repair rent flesh and shattered bone. Someone had removed Hugh's helm and had bathed his sweaty face. Faint starlight showed the deathly pallor tainting pale skin. Hugh would die, and Malcolm seethed with anger at his powerlessness to save him.

"We have not long to wait," Lulach whispered, so Hugh would not hear.

"Then we wait," Malcolm decided. He would let the young man, once so eager to serve beneath him, die in peace.

Hugh's fingers gripped his. "I fear I have done you shame. I am not the knight I prayed to be."

"Fear not, Hugh. You fought like a true warrior. I am proud of you."

"'Tis all I ever asked." Hugh let out a rasping breath, and Malcolm closed his eyes, unwilling to watch another fine man die.

Such was a knight's life, easily spent, easily expended, lost on a dark road for no reason. The injustice of it beat at him like a wielded spike, but there was naught Malcolm could do to change the way of the world or turn back the tide of death.

He had survived and was left to mourn—as always—those who did not.

"The young knight has fallen," Alma whispered as they galloped down the dark lane. "We must help him."

"He trussed me up like a pig. I'll not risk my freedom and welfare for any man." Elin thought of the dark, fierce knight and how he'd taunted her. And then of the younger knight, who had shown kindness toward Alma. "I shall not return."

Yet she slowed the mare from a gallop to a trot. Then she halted the animal entirely. What was her freedom worth? If the king wanted her at his court, then nothing would spare her. That little voice inside her head had been smiting her since she'd fled Hugh's watchful eye.

"'Tis an unwise decision," she informed Alma.

"But a noble course."

"Fie on nobility! The true reason I turn this palfrey around is so that I might sleep at night. I'll not have some man's death on my conscience!" Truly, she was no soft-hearted female. She could wield a sword as well as her brother and run twice as far. And a pox on anyone who thought her weak and sentimental.

They had escaped the moment Hugh had dropped hold of their reins to raise his sword in battle. Whoever challenged the king's knights could only mean more complications. 'Twas rumored few could outfight Malcolm the Fierce. Alma had refused to flee, but Elin could taste freedom. She did not trust even the king's knight to be true.

So she'd caught hold of the old woman's reins and galloped off into the night, unnoticed as the clash of steel and the roaring cries from bloodthirsty men rang in her ears. Only a fool would return.

Now, when she reached the last bend in the road, silence met her. Dark shadows revealed the forms of men kneeling in the way, forming a ring around a death-still body.

Unnoticed, Elin dismounted. Her limbs quaked with the act of walking back into the hands of her captors, whether they took her in good faith or bad, yet all she could see was Hugh. Too pale of face meant he had lost too much blood. She had seen that ashen sweat before in the gravely injured, as she had the shallow breathing and loss of consciousness.

There was little time if she held any hopes of saving his life.

"Are you men knotty-pated dolts? Hugh is cold. Fetch me some blankets. You, the tall one. Make a fire over there by the bank. Quickly now. Do not sit there staring at me."

The dark knight rose from the fallen Hugh's side. "Do as she bids, men."

He lumbered close, the jangle of his mail loud in her ears. He turned his forceful gaze upon her. "Have you healing knowledge?"

"More than most." She refused to tremble beneath the power of his scrutiny. "I need water boiled. You will see to it?"

"As you wish." He nodded and was gone, barking orders. Authority rang in his voice, in his manner. He was not just a man of war, but a commander of men.

She knelt beside the injured knight, clutching the few crocks of herbs she had in her possession. She reached beneath her mantle for the knife and bared it.

"Look! She has a weapon!" a man cried, and hard fingers imprisoned her wrist.

"Are you mad? Unhand me!" She looked up into eyes of the one who assisted le Farouche.

"Nay, I will not have you slit his throat, you witch."

"I am more likely to slit yours." She still gripped her knife and fought with muscle and strength to keep the much larger knight from forcibly lowering her arm.

"Release her, Giles." That dark voice was rich with both power and amusement. "I trust her to see to Hugh."

"She is a sorceress, sir, if she thinks she can bring back the dead."

"He is not dead. Yet. Merely unconscious. Leave me to my work," Elin demanded, her temper ready to flare. She had not returned for abuse, but to help the knight who had been kind to Alma.

"I share your suspicions, Giles." Teasing laughter filled that dark voice. "She does possess the unruly manner of a sorceress."

Elin did not think she could hate le Farouche more than

she did at that moment. She had given up her freedom and
mayhap her life for a hired killer's jesting? Fury drove her,
and she tore her hand free before the knight, Giles, released
her, earning his surprise and a nod of approval from le
Farouche.

Fie! As if she needed his approval.

"You." She pointed her blade at Malcolm. "Help me
with his armor, since you are the only man without work
to do."

"You despise my idleness?" He chuckled, deep and as
intriguing as midnight.

"That and more. Now, quickly. I must see the wound.
Use my blade." She jabbed the knife toward him, hilt first.

His big blunt fingers curled over the steel weapon, engulfing it. The thick blade appeared like a toy against his
powerful bulk. She shivered and bowed her head. She had
watched him slash the life from men she'd known much of
her life, men who had protected her while she rode the
countryside gathering her herbs.

Now, gazing up the length of the dark knight, she knew
some measure of fear. She felt the weight of his gaze, read
the cynical darkness in his eyes, hated the strength in his
craggy body. The latent power to kill rested in the thickness
of his arms and shoulders, chest and thighs.

He both took her breath away and made her blood run
cold. He was a beautiful masculine form. He was a destroyer of life. The irony beat at her. Truly this was the
epitome of man—a beautiful destroyer—and the reason she
both feared and hated men so.

"Do you think me a witch?" she demanded.

She watched Malcolm's impassive face, well molded
with high cheekbones and a straight blade of a nose. "Nay,
else you would have uttered spells and curses when I captured you. Instead, you relied on more honest weapons."

Her knife in his hand glinted once in the starlight, illuminating briefly the man kneeling beside her. His head bent with his work. She could see his black hair curling at his nape, could see the fine lines etched around his dark eyes, caused by time and war and too much sun. He was rumored to have fought in the Outremer, as her brother had. 'Twas unbelievable. This dark knight, as frightening as death and midnight, had fought for Christ?

Impossible. He had the coldness of a mercenary, the mockery of a knave and the… She hesitated, watching him separate the unconscious Hugh from his chain mail. He had the hands of a healer. They were strong and gentle, as if he was well acquainted with death and life. Nay, it could not be. Not this man.

The scent of freshly spilled blood reminded her of her purpose. She bent to remove the lids of her unmarked crocks and, because of the darkness, sniffed each one. She recognized the sharp smell of marigold. And then the sweet odor of camphor.

"Blankets." Giles returned, careful to keep his distance.

She took the wool coverings he offered and was not amused when the knight stepped back. Out of fear? Revulsion? She noticed now that others did the same, suspicion written on their shadowed faces. The same suspicions she always raised when she acted differently from the obedient baron's daughter they expected. Fie on them! As if she could sit at embroidery all day without going insane. Men did not do it. Why should she?

"Do you wish him covered?" Malcolm's voice drew her back to the task before her.

Now that Hugh was free of his armor, she could begin her work. "Aye. First I want him off this cold ground. Spread out one length of wool, and you and I together will lift him onto it."

"You and I?" He crooked his brow skeptically.

"How stupid of me to forget my lack of muscle! I will just have to try all the harder. Now, grab his head. Lift him gently on count of three."

"Let one of my knights…"

Elin was used to the foolish beliefs of men. She grabbed Hugh's ankles firmly, eyeing the stain of blood from his neck to his groin. A mortal wound. Sadness filled her. At least Hugh was unconscious and out of his misery. 'Twas always her patient's pain that caused her the most sorrow. "One, two, three," she counted, and lifted.

As le Farouche hurried to secure Hugh's head, knights rushed to Elin's side, obviously doubting her strength. But she lifted Hugh almost as easily as the fierce knight did, and when they laid the injured man on the warm blanket, she saw the approval in Malcolm's eyes—eyes like night without shadows. Light from the nearby fire chased away the deepest shades of darkness, giving more shape and substance to the knight. Dried blood marked his face in two places, above his brow and on his swollen lower lip. He was injured, but she read in his actions, on his face that he thought only of the one gravely wounded.

"Looks like a deep gash to his abdomen. 'Tis not good." She probed the wound with careful fingers. Blood rushed from the raw cavity. She scented severed intestines. "Alma, I shall need bandages and a good light."

"Giles," Malcolm ordered. "Bring a torch."

In seconds a torch on a long handle was impaled in the ground at her side, revealing without remorse the neat and terrible wound. "I need to stop the blood first."

"There's naught you can do." Worry and regret weighed down le Farouche's words. "Unless you truly are a sorceress."

"I have been called worse." She thanked Alma for the

needle and thread. The old woman hurried away to make ready bandages and to check on the water's progress. "Take my knife and cut his flesh here. And here." She pulled at the raw skin at the edges of the wound.

"I'll not worsen it."

"Then I will." She snatched at the knife he held, but his fingers of steel would not release it. "I do not know if I can save him," Elin confessed. "I have lost men injured far less seriously. But if I cannot bind the entrails and stem the source of blood, there will be certain death."

"You cannot be a healer. No one claiming to cure would carve a deeper wound."

"Then let your friend die. But know this, le Farouche— Sir Hugh's death will not be on my conscience, but on yours."

Chapter Three

Hugh would soon be dead, Malcolm knew, but the maiden's challenge goaded him. Regardless if he allowed her to continue her ghastly work, his conscience would never forgive this senseless death. He had failed to protect the young knight, a responsibility he felt toward each and every man who fought at his side, who willingly risked their lives at his command.

The old woman ambled forward with a trencher of steaming water and a pile of torn undergarments. "Shall I soak the bandages?"

The girl nodded. She looked like a witch—not knobby nosed and wart ridden, but different from most women. Strong willed, the way a man was. And strong of body. He'd had difficulty keeping hold of the knife when she'd tried to take it from him, and 'twas amazing how easily she lifted half of Hugh's weight. A sorceress, Giles had declared.

Hugh lay dying, his face a deathly gray. Soon he would bleed to death. Malcolm would have to trust her. His experience told him to be wary of women holding knives, women who gazed at him with that confident knowledge of a battle-experienced leader. Her strength beguiled him, contrasting sharply with the fragile cut of her face, at once beautiful and innocent; to her lithe grace and womanly curves. Truly such a sorceress could enchant a man. Or worse.

Yet she gazed at him with human eyes, waiting patiently for control of her knife. He saw in those blue depths a wise purpose. She had healed others gravely wounded before. He could read her confidence in her stance, feel it like an imminent storm on the wind—half instinct, half experience, but certain.

He'd seen evil, and it was not Elinore of Evenbough.

He released her knife. "Do what you must. But I will have you know Hugh was my friend."

"I will do him no harm, fierce one." She was young to be so confident, but her words eased his fears. She tapped herbs from a small crock into the steaming water and then dipped her blade into the mixture. "I learned my meager healing arts from a wise woman. She was skilled in anatomy and cures."

Malcolm's stomach turned as Elin slipped the blade into the red-edged flesh and tore widthwise across the gaping slash. The skin opened wider, like a hungry mouth. Blood rushed with renewed fury, and he almost stayed the girl-woman's hand.

"I was not surprised to return and see your knights victorious." She soaked strips of cloth in the trencher, then stuffed them into Hugh's wound. They became colored with blood. "Tell me what fearsome enemy of the king's you have overpowered now. An old man? Mayhap a lame woman? A goat?"

"Take care, dove, else you shall offend."

"'Tis good to know I come close to succeeding."

He snorted. What manner of woman was this Elin of Evenbough? He believed women should be tamed like a good horse, bridled and saddled and prepared to answer a man's command, and this girl was not. Yet he couldn't deny a grudging respect for her. She did not flinch as he did at the sight of the wound. He was used to inflicting them, not studying them.

"See, there is much damage." She removed the cloths and probed the pink cavity with knowing fingers. "I note two tears, here and here. Look how deep they are."

"I prefer not."

She laughed. "Can it be such a great warrior has a weak stomach? Aye, 'tis not pretty to see the damage done by a man's violent sword."

He heard the censure in that and chose to remain silent. She had returned of her own accord—why, he could not fathom. Surely not to heal a fallen man, one she had not thought twice about kicking like an angry donkey. Yet Malcolm could not deny her touch was tender and her intent to heal sincere. She stitched and cleaned, studied her work, then stitched some more. Beads of sweat dotted her forehead and dampened the tendrils of gold gathered there, curling them, though the night was cold.

He could not deny how hard she worked. And for what? This daughter of a traitor ought to be bound like her father to a tree. She ought to fear for the crimes she faced. And yet she saw only Hugh and uttered commands to the old woman as if she were a king at war.

Light brushed her face, soft as the fine weave of her gown and cloak, stained by travel. 'Twas a pretty face, not beautiful, but striking. She had big, almond-shaped eyes, blue like winter, direct, not coy. Long curled lashes, as gold as her hair, framed those eyes. He admired her gently sloping, feminine nose. And her mouth! God's teeth, 'twas bow shaped and as tempting as that of the moon goddess herself.

Then Elin sighed, a soft release of air, all emotion, all

sadness. Her unblinking gaze collided with his directly; there was no flirting, no shyness, no feminine submission. "I fear there is more damage than I can repair, but the wound, both inside and out, is closed."

He swallowed. "Hugh will die?"

"There's no fever yet." She laid a small hand to the unconscious knight's forehead. "A fine sign. Now we must pray he is strong enough. I will do all I can."

"You will, because I command it." She may have returned of her own volition, but Elin of Evenbough was his prisoner still. He would not fail his king.

A smile tugged at one corner of her mouth, and that defiant chin firmed. "Again you try to terrify me, a woman half your size. Always the valiant warrior."

Anger snapped in his chest and he held his tongue. She challenged his authority; she rebelled at something deeper. He was, as she said, twice her size and twice her strength. And he had her knife—her last one, he guessed—in his keeping. The only weapon left her was her tongue, and he could withstand those barbs. And if not, he would gag her, as he had her betrothed, the treacherous Caradoc.

"Old woman." He caught the crone's gaze, and she trembled at the attention. Though old and stooped, she possessed a strong set to her jaw, too. "See that your charge tends the injured men, mine and those captured. But not her father. Let the man suffer like the men he left to die."

"Yes, Sir Malcolm. I will see the rebellious one obeys." Head bowed, she scurried away.

Malcolm stepped away into the darkness. The wee hours of morning meant there would be little, mayhap no sleep for him before dawn. And then another day of raising his sword for the king.

Elin of Evenbough had the freedom to speak as she wished, whether innocent or criminal. But Caradoc was right. Malcolm was a peasant born, a barbarian king's bastard, and both peasant and bastard he would always be. A savage hired merely because he was useful. Useful until another took his place, his livelihood or his head.

He thought of Caradoc's threat, thought of the unrest of ambitious knights wanting to lead, thought of Elin's courage in returning to aid her captors.

Lavender light chased the gray shadows at the eastern horizon. 'Twould be another day without peace, without rest, watching his back for treachery and the road ahead for danger.

The lot of a knight was a hard one, but Malcolm was harder.

"Caradoc!" Elin dropped to her knees before the bound man, neighbor and friend to her father. "I do not believe my eyes. What have you done? Challenged the king's knights and lost?"

He colored from the collar of his hauberk to the roots of his dark hair. "Aye. Your father—"

"You are in league with my father?" she yelped, lowering her voice so it would not carry to the watchful knight keeping guard. That Giles, he looked untrustworthy, far more threatening than poor spying Hugh had ever been.

"Nay, I am no traitor. I would never turn against the king. I came for you."

"Me?"

"My future bride." Triumph glittered in his cold eyes.

"'Tis news to me." She fought to sound unaffected. Surely this man dreamed! By the rood, she would no more marry him than Malcolm le Farouche.

"Your father and I had exchanged words on the matter."

"We are not betrothed and you know it, Caradoc." She swiped a clean cloth through the steaming trencher.

''We could be.''

''You only covet my father's holdings, else you would not risk your life, your freedom and your barony.''

''Your father offered you to me.''

''I am not a cow to be bought and sold.'' She brushed at the bloody but shallow cut beneath his jaw. ''Look at this wound. Put there by le Farouche's sword.''

''Loosen my bonds and I will kill him for you. For your honor.''

''Do not do my name that injustice. You would kill him for your uses, not mine, if you could.''

''He defeated me unfairly.''

''Most likely the unfair warrior was you.'' Elin knew Caradoc, not by rumor, but from experience. He despised her, as she did him. Worse, she was afraid of him. Hard and dark were his eyes, not lethal like Malcolm's, but colder still, like a man who killed for pleasure.

As she thought of Malcolm, she looked up and saw him, a fierce knight shrouded in darkness and shadow, standing away from the shivering light of the fire and torch, alone with the night. He had removed his helm, and the wind moved through his long tresses, which were as black as the night. His gaze fastened on hers, and she read his suspicions like a thought in her own mind. As if he were part of her, or she part of him.

Traitor. Malcolm thought her guilty of her father's crimes. She shivered inside as he strode toward her. He moved like a predator, with silent, powerful strides, until he towered overhead, all tensed male might.

''Do you conspire with this man, this suspected traitor?''

She blanched. ''Caradoc is no traitor! Do you accuse every man, woman and child?''

''Silence. I forbid you to speak further with this unworthy lord.'' Le Farouche's lethal look came as a warning.

Yet two different responses sparked to life in her breast. Fear, because she knew Alma was wrong: the fierce knight had his own dark agenda, and Elin knew now to be wary of it. And a light, hot flutter of attraction, because his steely presence stole the very breath from her lungs and stilled the blood in her veins. She fought this response to him. No man of war and killing could attract her. Not even a man this compelling, this beautifully made.

"'Tis just as well, for I will have naught more to do with Ravenwood." Let le Farouche think she was following his bidding. She had her own reasons for keeping distance between herself and Caradoc. "May I tend my father now that I have treated all other manner of men?"

"You have yet to tend me." Brows arched across his blade-sharp gaze.

"I refuse to touch the likes of you." Elin lifted her chin, certain now of the danger she was in. "Even a lowly woman unable to bear weapons has her standards." She rose.

The fierce knight towered over her, as immovable as a great stone mountain. His mouth twisted when he spoke, mayhap in anger. "Tempt me any further, maid, and I will care naught for your skills to heal, and bind you to a tree like the rest of the traitors."

"Then bind yourself as well, for you keep to your own agenda in holding captive whomever you come across, be it lord or unarmed woman." She balanced the trencher so as not to spill it. Curls of steam rose in the chilly dawn air. "I will tend my father."

"I say you shall not." His grimace flashed in the waning darkness. "Try me no further."

"What will you do? Slay me here in the road? 'Tis better than waiting for the same fate in London." Fear trembled through her, for she was no fool. She heard both anger and truth rumbling in that voice.

"You think I will strike you down?" he roared. "Have I raised my sword to you? Have I struck you? Ravished you? Given you to my men to suit their pleasures?"

She felt small as his wrath filled him, making him seem taller, larger. The air vibrated with his keen male power, and she shivered. "I cannot say you have."

"Nor will I, on my honor." He spat the words, and fire-light caught on the steel hilt of his sword, glinting with a reminder of his undefeatable strength. "You have endured no more than being carried from the woods and forced to ride with us. Do you think your betrothed, Ravenwood, would be less cruel?"

"He is not my betrothed," she declared savagely. If she married the man, 'twould be like ordering her own death. "Never call him that to my face."

"The maiden warrior is not so easily bent. Do you not fear me?"

He leaned close. She saw the flash of black eyes and white teeth and the hard demanding countenance of a man used to leading battles, of a man used to facing death. She shivered again. "I both fear and loathe you, sir."

"A true answer, at last. I despise liars, dove. And the company they keep."

"As do I."

"Then keep this in mind." His gaze bored into her, as sharp as any dagger. She stepped back, but he followed, intent upon dominating her as a wolf stalks wounded prey. "I despise your sharp tongue and your rebellious ways, and 'tis clear your father failed to beat you properly."

"Beat me?" She seethed. What was this? "A knight such as you would surely think violence is the greatest teacher."

"What I think matters naught. Only how the king judges you. Keep this in mind, fighting dove. I tell no lies to my king. If Edward asks if you fought, if you lacked respect, if you gave any indication you were guilty, then I will tell him what has transpired between us."

"You would condemn me either way."

"Nay. Only you have that power."

She shivered yet again. The threat of such a future felt real for the first time. In Malcolm's eyes, she could see the grim reality ahead. Would she truly be seated before the king and judged a traitor?

"I am a terrible daughter for certain," she confessed. Everyone from the lowliest peasant farmer to the highest knight would agree. "But I am loyal. To friend, family and country. Believe me, or condemn an innocent."

One corner of his mouth quirked. "I am not your judge, Elin of Evenbough."

"Do you mock me?" There, on his bloody swollen lip, shone the barest hint of laughter. "Does talk of an unjust traitor's punishment amuse you?"

"Nay." That humor waned, as silent as the night. "You amuse me—the cruel world does not. Take care in how you act from this moment on. You have tended my men. That will serve you well in the king's court. I will tell how you worked of your own free will until day's light without food or water or rest."

"I came to tend Hugh. I shall not have a dead man on my conscience. I returned to care for his wound, not to prove my innocence or earn a better judgment from the king."

"You *ought* to worry about proof, or you will watch your entrails be cut from your body as they draw and quarter you. I have seen enough of such punishment to know it one of the cruelest. You will be alive when they begin butchering you. Remember, innocent or guilty, all that matters is proof of innocence.''

"And I have no proof, no lies to cover, no one to bribe, no way to show I know what my father plotted.''

"You know he plotted?''

"He plots constantly. And as he sits weeping there in the shadows, he still plots a way to escape.'' Tears knotted her throat and she fell silent. Anger, fear and an enormous chill of betrayal cloaked her body. What had her father done, involving her in his escape? Had she known he sought to evade the king's protector, she would have held fast to her bedpost and refused to let go.

Now she would face court. With no way to prove her innocence, save Caradoc, the king's nephew, trussed up to an oak tree. She could not ask his help. Not from a cheater, a killer and a wife beater. To enlist his aid would mean she would have to agree to his outrageous claims of marriage.

What she needed was a plot of her own. She needed to avoid the king's court, Caradoc's influence and the strong sword of Malcolm le Farouche. Already the lavender tint to the horizon began fading to peach. Soon the sun would rise, and they would journey toward London and her fate as a traitor's daughter.

An idea came to her, and she could not take time to think through the consequences. Being kind to the fierce one would not be easy, though she vowed to do it. For both her life and her freedom. "You bleed, sir.''

"What? No insults? No name-calling? Not 'sirrah,' or 'cowardly knave'?''

Let him mock her. He might be twice as strong, but she was twice as smart. "Nay, I must apologize for my disrespect. You speak truth. I have a rebellious nature, but I have neither the power nor the will to conspire against the king. I will seek to show from this moment forth that I am innocent, and each action will prove this to you and to the king.''

"Well chosen. I will do all I can to aid your cause, for you have given all to tend my wounded men.'' The frown faded from his mouth. Though he did not smile, she saw a glimmer of kindness, another puzzle to this man of steel and might. "How fares Hugh?''

"He lives yet.'' She selected a clean cloth from the many slung over her shoulder and dipped it into the trencher she held. She stepped close to him—close enough to inhale his night forest and man scent, to feel the heat from his body and see the stubbled growth on his jaw. She dabbed at the cut to his lip and he winced, but did not step away. "Hugh cannot be moved.''

"We cannot remain here.'' He gestured with an upturned palm at the road.

"To move your knight is to kill him. He must remain still for the stitched wounds inside to heal. Else I guarantee he will bleed to death. I recall a village not a league from here. It must have an inn. I believe Sir Hugh can travel that far.''

Malcolm caught her hand, his fingers curling around her wrist and forcing the cloth from his face. The power of his gaze, unbending and lethal as the steel sword at his belt, speared her.

"Is this a plot?'' he demanded. "Are you attempting to fool me into a trap you and your lover have devised?''

"Lover? You mean Caradoc?'' Outrage knifed through her. "What has that addlepated knave told you?''

"Only that he is your betrothed.'' Was that amusement she saw flash in his dark eyes?

"As I said, 'tis untrue. He covets my father's holdings. Seeing him bound like a scoundrel gives me great pleasure.''

Malcolm laughed, the sound rich and friendly this time, not mocking. "You need not tend my wounds, dove. They will heal in time. Day breaks. See to Hugh and prepare him for travel. We will leave him at this inn you know of. If I spy any act of treachery, I will chain you to the wall of the king's dungeon myself."

Aye, but you will never be able to find me. Fear trembled through her, and yet she forced a smile to her lips. Her heart thumped with some unnatural reaction to this man of sword and death, dark like the shadows even as the sun rose and brought light to the world.

Chapter Four

A sense of doom settled in Malcolm's chest as he watched three of his knights lay an unconscious Hugh upon a rickety bed covered in fresh linen. He did not care what the traitor's daughter predicted. They had brought Hugh here to die.

Malcolm could not stomach how he'd failed the young knight, who'd often proclaimed his eagerness to serve his king and fight beneath the Fierce One's command. Bitterness soured Malcolm's mouth.

"I'll need hot water. You—" Elin pointed a slim finger at one of his men "—see to it."

"Dove, these are *my* men to command. Lulach, Hugh needs fresh water. We cannot send the traitor's daughter for it."

"True." Anger burned in resentful eyes, for Lulach, as Malcolm suspected others did, blamed Elin and her father for Hugh's injuries. "I'll go, but make no mistake. I'm no criminal woman's handmaiden."

Malcolm watched Elin of Evenbough blanch, and saw the denial sharpen her face. She muttered something beneath her breath—and he knew he would have objected had he heard it—then she knelt gracefully at Hugh's side.

The poor knight's chances were not good; Malcolm

knew this even before she rolled back layers of wool and linen. A neatly stitched gash stretched from Hugh's ribs to his groin. She bent to study it, her golden hair, with a hint of red, like a flame that caught and shimmered in the sunlight slanting through the open door. She was liquid fire, and when she tilted her face up to meet his gaze, his chest burned as if a firestorm raged there, wicked and untamed.

"I see no sign of fever. Look, no redness marks the edges of the wound." A measure of joy filled her voice. Not triumph or pride, for Malcolm knew those well enough, but gladness. And her gladness surprised him. "I predict Hugh will live."

"Do you always predict what you cannot control?"

"What? You doubt my abilities?"

"Aye, I doubt all women." The girl was too green. She'd not seen death and dying the way he had. A gray pallor clung to the wounded man's face and took hold, growing stronger as the light shifted and deepened.

"Truly, a man such as you sees naught but dying. What do you know of the living?" She turned her shoulder to him, as if he'd insulted her.

He could not argue. For once the dove was correct.

"Where's Alma?" Her low voice wobbled a bit.

"I sent her to aid the innkeeper's wife, who is crippled with joint pain. They are not accustomed to receiving so many men at once. 'Tis a small village, and these roads not often traveled. Only a traitor evading the king's knights might choose this path."

"You needn't remind me of my plight." Elin bowed her head, searching through the satchel she carried. Crocks clattered together, and the dull clunks and thunks chimed noisily in the somber tension of the air. "Bring me Alma."

"Nay, dove. If you need assistance, I shall give it."

"You?" Her eyes widened, and she lifted one corner of

her mouth in disbelief. Then, mayhap remembering her vow to behave, she erased that sneer from her delicate lips, pearled with early morning light. "You admit you know naught of healing."

"I can hold a trencher well enough." He hid his chuckle behind a cough, amused at her valiant effort not to insult him. Aye, the poor girl was trying, but like an untamed horse facing the prospect of a saddle, she could not hide her unwillingness. "Besides, you are my prisoner. I'll not leave your side, traitor's daughter."

Temper flared in her eyes, glaring like sunlight on water. Her fists curled, but no anger sounded in her voice. She was like any woman, always pretending. "I will honor your offer of assistance, for you are the greatest knight in all the realm."

"Not so great." He waited, and although he sensed them, no insults spewed from her sharp tongue. He accepted the trencher of steaming water Lulach handed him. "I've seen many manner of men, dove, and not one has been so noble as to bear that title."

"In this we agree." She tapped herbs into the water, her gaze avoiding his. "Do you think the king will believe Caradoc's claim?"

"I cannot say. The king has a mind of his own, though he's known to be fair. It depends on your father. Whether he chooses to speak the truth, or if he is swayed by Caradoc's false promises to help save him."

"Caradoc, aye, he is my fear." She dipped the cloth into the trencher, leaning close. Her delicately shaped mouth frowned as she worked, and with it her entire face. Soft lines eased across her brow and crinkled at the corners of her eyes. His gaze flickered across the cut of her lips.

Aye, she was young, far too spirited for his taste and

much too soft. Yet his chest tightened, and air caught with a painful hitch between his ribs.

"Caradoc is a man of much weakness, many lies," he admitted.

"What? You believe me? That I am not betrothed to him?" Her measuring gaze latched on to his.

He could see the intelligence in those eyes, the thoughts forming behind them. "I know the like of Ravenwood far too well. I've seen many brutes of that ilk."

"He's nephew to the king."

"Aye. I'm well acquainted with that fact."

Hugh murmured, as if fighting to awaken. Malcolm reached for his hand so the young knight would know he was not alone. But Elin's fingers were already there, and her compassion glimmered, as unmistakable as the steady glow of sunlight into the dim room. Hugh quieted, and she continued her work bathing his wound.

"Then he will awaken?"

"Aye." She cast Malcolm a mischievous smile, quick and fleeting. "You doubt my knowledge, but you'll soon see. Hugh will live."

"Then he'll owe his life to you."

"Nay, to Alma. *She* pecked like a troubled conscience until I had to return to aid him."

But Malcolm knew the truth when he saw it. "Nay, I think you returned to aid your betrothed."

She sparkled with humor. "Go ahead, tease. You shall see what a sacrifice I made in returning, once you spend an entire day with Caradoc. Your knights are likely to behead him just to stop his insults."

"Does he cast an insult more sharp than yours?"

She almost laughed, and with the sunlight alive in her fiery curls, she was transformed before his eyes into a nymph of beauty and mischief. "I admit I studied Caradoc's skill, for although I hate the man, I do admire his foul temper.''

"'Tis a skill you practice then? Like wielding a sword?''

"Aye. I am a woman who does both.''

He laughed. How this girl-woman amused him. He'd not been amused by much in more years than he could count. He handed her a fresh bandage when she gestured for one. "Caradoc is trussed up in the stable under guard. At last report, he still had his head.''

Elin gazed at Malcolm with that fire flickering in her eyes, as mesmerizing as a mirage in the desert, when heat and earth and imagination created illusions. "Will the king judge me innocent of treason, but condemn me in marriage to his nephew?''

"'Tis more likely than Edward deciding to have you hanged, drawn and quartered.'' A warning twisted in Malcolm's guts and prickled along the back of his neck. "As long as you continue to prove your innocence to me, you will live.''

"You are not my judge.''

"Nay, but I am your jailer.''

But not for long. Elin thought of the dried oakwood tucked into a pouch in one of her herb crocks. Even a small amount of the berry could render a grown man ill for hours. Ill enough to allow her escape.

Malcolm caught hold of her hand, his big callused fingers rough and strangely fascinating as they covered hers. "Quit your worries, dove. Edward will be pleased that you saved young Hugh's life.''

For a brief instant she saw behind the heartless eyes, to the ghost of the man he must have once been before he turned killer and traded his soul for the coin it would bring.

'Twas almost a shame she'd have to poison him. But

death or marriage to Caradoc? She would not go quietly toward either darkness.

"The crone is serving Giles and the prisoners in the stable. The innkeeper's wife could not do it." Lulach settled on the bench and quickly drained the tankard of ale. "I must hurry, ere the old woman begins a plot to free the traitors."

"Rest and eat, the crone will cause no trouble." Malcolm took his eating knife from his belt. "'Tis the younger one we must watch."

"She is a witch, that one. Able to defeat us with her spells and powers."

"Nay, she's no sorceress. Look how she works." He gestured to the young woman emerging from the kitchen, steaming trenchers in hand, her fine wool mantle shivering around her slim thighs with every step she took.

Lulach growled, still disbelieving. "Beware she does not cast a spell over our meal and sicken us."

"I've seen sorcery, and 'tis not what the traitor woman practices with her simple herbs." Any memories of the Outremer filled Malcolm with blackness and horror. He forced those images to the back of his mind. "But still, I trust her not."

"'Tis wise." Lulach carefully studied the food Elin had helped prepare after tending Hugh.

"More mead?" The dove's voice sang as pleasantly as a morning breeze. With a smile, she handed Malcolm a second tankard.

The back of his neck crawled. Aye, he could sense she was up to no good. When they departed after the meal, he would tie her again to the saddle. While he could not bear to leave Hugh, his king expected the traitor without delay.

They would have to leave the injured man behind. The life of a knight was not fair.

"Elin?" He caught the female by the elbow, and she turned to him with concern in her eyes.

"What is it, le Farouche? Is it the food—"

"Nay. I am considering asking Alma to stay with…" His stomach twisted, and he placed a hand there.

An agonized groan sounded in the room behind him, rumbling like a thunderclap. Another groan was followed by an unpleasant sound.

"She's poisoned us!" Giles accused, arriving breathless in the doorway. Sunlight shifted around his form and betrayed how he trembled. "Men are dropping like flies in the stable. Even the prisoners. Look, I begin to sweat."

Discord rose as rough shouts and threats resonated in the smoke-ridden air. As if she was guilty, Elin's eyes widened and she spun away. Malcolm reached out and snared her by the sleeve, but only briefly.

"Silence," he roared, temper raging with the force of a storm at sea. His stomach squeezed again, and he fell to his knees. "Lady Elinore, what have you done?"

"What I had to do." She laid a hand on his forehead, a touch of compassion. Her caress soothed like water against the shore.

"Kill the king's men, and you'll pay with more than just your life." He tried to climb to his knees, but his senses spun. His vision blurred. He remained crouched like a dog upon the earthen floor.

"The poison is not a lethal dose. I was careful. Do not fret, Sir Malcolm. You'll live."

A sick taste filled his mouth. Strength seeped from his limbs until he could only lie motionless in the dirt. "Then when this poison loosens its hold on me, believe this. I will hunt you down. You cannot hide from me."

"I can try." She knelt over him and took the dagger from his belt. He saw her soft leather boots, small and finely tailored, as she stepped over him.

"Elin!" he shouted. "Do not do this! I beg of you."

But the tap of her step against dirt and stone faded away into nothing, nothing at all.

She was gone, the vile betrayer, and he wretched, groaning in misery.

He would hunt her down. Malcolm the Fierce would not rest until he had the traitor woman's head.

"I cannot leave." Alma dug in her heels. "There is Hugh to think of. And look, these men will need an herbed tea to calm their stomachs."

"Nay, I want their stomachs churning." Elin gave the cinch a good pull. "Listen, only danger lies ahead for me."

"Danger?"

"Why did Father bring us on this journey? We have no explanation. Perchance he planned something sinister. Then innocent protestations will not save us."

"What if justice prevails? I see no danger then."

"Not for you. But Father's barony may be lost, and who will be at court to beg favors from Edward? Caradoc. He claims we are betrothed, and there will be no debate. Why should the king not secure the barony with his own blood?"

"'Tis logic you speak. And truth." Alma frowned, her brows drawn together in serious thought. "Yet I cannot leave Hugh. He needs much care."

"Aye. It weighs heavily on my conscience." Elin rubbed her forehead, then turned to her waiting palfrey.

"Elin!" 'Twas Caradoc's voice, thin with sickness. "You've not fallen ill from this vile food. Free me, and I'll take these black knights to Edward's punishment."

Alarm beat in her chest. She leaned close, whispering to

Alma. "See what he plans? There still remains doubt over
the true cause of his wife's death. Can you blame me?"

"Nay. Do as you must." Troubled, Alma laid her hand
over the cross at her neck. "Promise to take care. I love
you as a daughter and could not bear to lose you." Tears
misted the old woman's eyes.

And burned in Elin's throat. "You've been a mother to
me, Alma. If le Farouche harms you, he will answer to me,
king's protector or nay."

"Aye, fierce you are." Alma's affection whispered in
her voice, soft like an east wind. She lifted the chain from
her neck. The silver cross, hand hewn, caught a flash of
sunlight from a crack in the roof.

"Nay, I cannot—"

"Take this with my blessing. 'Twill bring you safely to
Elizabeth's." She secured the chain around Elin's neck,
tears on her face. "My prayers are with you."

"Then I have all I need." Elin pressed a kiss to Alma's
papery cheek, and then mounted the waiting palfrey before
she could change her mind.

She was not sentimental, not one bit, but leaving Alma
made her heart ache. As she galloped past the inn, she saw
the wide-open door and thought of Malcolm within, the
fiercest of knights who now suffered by her hand.

She didn't like what she had done, but she could not
depend upon a knight without heart or soul, without mercy
or conscience to save her, to plead her cause, to protect her
from Caradoc before the king. Malcolm was more shadow
than substance, more killer than man.

Yet she'd seen the pain on his face when she'd taken his
dagger. He hurt in the way of a real man.

Giles leaned against the door frame, sagging from weakness. "She left the prisoners."